THIS BOOK

BELONGS TO:

....

....

THE STORY OF
Miss Moppet

THE STORY OF
MISS MOPPET

BY

BEATRIX POTTER

A PETER RABBIT™

110th Anniversary Edition

FREDERICK WARNE

FREDERICK WARNE

Published by the Penguin Group
Penguin Books Ltd., 80 Strand, London WC2R 0RL, England
Penguin Group (USA) Inc., 375 Hudson Street, New York, New York 10014, USA
Penguin Group (Australia), 250 Camberwell Road, Camberwell,
Victoria 3124, Australia (a division of Pearson Australia Group Pty. Ltd.)
Penguin Group (Canada), 90 Eglinton Avenue East, Suite 700, Toronto,
Ontario M4P 2Y3, Canada (a division of Pearson Penguin Canada Inc.)
Penguin Books India Pvt. Ltd., 11 Community Centre, Panchsheel Park, New Delhi—110 017, I
Penguin Books (NZ), 67 Apollo Drive, Rosedale, Auckland 0632,
New Zealand (a division of Pearson New Zealand Ltd.)
Penguin Books (South Africa) (Pty.) Ltd, 24 Sturdee Avenue, Rosebank, Johannesburg 2196, South A

Penguin Books Ltd., Registered Offices: 80 Strand, London WC2R 0RL, England

Website: www.peterrabbit.com

First published by Frederick Warne in 1906
First published with reset text and new reproductions
of Beatrix Potter's illustrations in 2002
This edition published in 2011

003 - 10 9 8 7 6 5 4 3

Colour reproduction by
EAE Creative Colour Ltd, Norwich
Printed and bound in China

PUBLISHER'S NOTE

The background to *The Story of Miss Moppet* is a sad one, as it was written shortly after the death of Beatrix Potter's editor and fiancé, Norman Warne. In the following year, she threw herself into work on three titles for babies that were to be published by Frederick Warne & Co. in an innovative concertina format.

The Story of Miss Moppet and *The Story of A Fierce Bad Rabbit* appeared in November 1906, but while the art and stories were widely admired, the complex format was a failure. In an era before shrink-wrapping, customers would open the concertina in the shop, then find it impossible to refold neatly and so render the book damaged and unsaleable. Fortunately, Warne & Co. republished both books in conventional forms in 1916 and they have continued to be enjoyed ever since.

THIS IS A PUSSY called Miss Moppet, she thinks she has heard a mouse!

THIS is the Mouse peeping out
behind the cupboard, and making
fun of Miss Moppet. He is not
afraid of a kitten.

THIS is Miss Moppet jumping just too late; she misses the Mouse and hits her own head.

SHE thinks it is a very hard
cupboard!

THE Mouse watches Miss Moppet from the top of the cupboard.

MISS MOPPET ties up her head in a duster, and sits before the fire.

THE Mouse thinks she is looking
very ill. He comes sliding down
the bell-pull.

19

MISS MOPPET looks worse and worse. The Mouse comes a little nearer.

MISS MOPPET holds her poor
head in her paws, and looks at
him through a hole in the duster.
The Mouse comes *very* close.

AND then all of a sudden —
Miss Moppet jumps upon the
Mouse!

AND because the Mouse has teased Miss Moppet — Miss Moppet thinks she will tease the Mouse; which is not at all nice of Miss Moppet.

SHE ties him up in the duster,
and tosses it about like a ball.

BUT she forgot about that hole in the duster; and when she untied it — there was no Mouse!

HE has wriggled out and run away; and he is dancing a jig on the top of the cupboard!

THE END

THIS BOOK

BELONGS TO:

Klara

THE TALE OF
Benjamin Bunny

THE TALE OF
BENJAMIN BUNNY

BY

BEATRIX POTTER

A PETER RABBIT™

110th Anniversary Edition

FREDERICK WARNE

FOR THE CHILDREN OF SAWREY
FROM OLD MR. BUNNY

FREDERICK WARNE

Published by the Penguin Group
Penguin Books Ltd., 80 Strand, London WC2R 0RL, England
Penguin Group (USA) Inc., 375 Hudson Street, New York, New York 10014, USA
Penguin Group (Australia), 250 Camberwell Road, Camberwell,
Victoria 3124, Australia (a division of Pearson Australia Group Pty. Ltd.)
Penguin Group (Canada), 90 Eglinton Avenue East, Suite 700, Toronto,
Ontario M4P 2Y3, Canada (a division of Pearson Penguin Canada Inc.)
Penguin Books India Pvt. Ltd., 11 Community Centre, Panchsheel Park, New Delhi—110 017, I
Penguin Group (NZ), 67 Apollo Drive, Rosedale, Auckland 0632,
New Zealand (a division of Pearson New Zealand Ltd.)
Penguin Books (South Africa) (Pty.) Ltd, 24 Sturdee Avenue, Rosebank, Johannesburg 2196, South A

Penguin Books Ltd., Registered Offices: 80 Strand, London WC2R 0RL, England

Website: www.peterrabbit.com

First published by Frederick Warne in 1904
First published with reset text and new reproductions
of Beatrix Potter's illustrations in 2002
This edition published in 2011

003 - 10 9 8 7 6 5 4 3

Colour reproduction by
EAE Creative Colour Ltd, Norwich
Printed and bound in China

PUBLISHER'S NOTE

Shortly before her second and third books *The Tale of Squirrel Nutkin* and *The Tailor of Gloucester* were published, Beatrix Potter began to worry about their reception. Perhaps they were 'too ingenious and complicated compared with Peter Rabbit,' she wrote to Frederick Warne & Co., her publisher. 'Don't you think the next one ought to be more simple?'

She sent rough ideas for a number of stories to her editor Norman Warne for his consideration, and the resulting project was *The Tale of Benjamin Bunny*, published along with *The Tale of Two Bad Mice* in September 1904. 'Miss Potter's fancy is not what it was,' grumbled the *Times Literary Supplement*, but the public begged to differ, and the book was an instant hit.

ONE MORNING a little rabbit sat on a bank.

He pricked his ears and listened to the trit-trot, trit-trot of a pony.

A gig was coming along the road; it was driven by Mr. McGregor, and beside him sat Mrs. McGregor in her best bonnet.

As soon as they had passed, little Benjamin Bunny slid down into the road, and set off — with a hop, skip and a jump — to call upon his relations, who lived in the wood at the back of Mr. McGregor's garden.

THAT wood was full of rabbit-holes; and in the neatest sandiest hole of all, lived Benjamin's aunt and his cousins — Flopsy, Mopsy, Cotton-tail and Peter.

Old Mrs. Rabbit was a widow; she earned her living by knitting rabbit-wool mittens and muffetees (I once bought a pair at a bazaar). She also sold herbs, and rosemary tea, and rabbit-tobacco (which is what *we* call lavender).

LITTLE Benjamin did not very much want to see his Aunt.

He came round the back of the fir-tree, and nearly tumbled upon the top of his Cousin Peter.

PETER was sitting by himself. He looked poorly, and was dressed in a red cotton pocket-handkerchief.

"Peter,"—said little Benjamin, in a whisper — "who has got your clothes?"

PETER replied—"The scarecrow in Mr. McGregor's garden," and described how he had been chased about the garden, and had dropped his shoes and coat.

Little Benjamin sat down beside his cousin, and assured him that Mr. McGregor had gone out in a gig, and Mrs. McGregor also; and certainly for the day, because she was wearing her best bonnet.

PETER said he hoped that it would rain.

At this point, old Mrs. Rabbit's voice was heard inside the rabbit-hole, calling — "Cotton-tail! Cotton-tail! fetch some more camomile!"

Peter said he thought he might feel better if he went for a walk.

THEY went away hand in hand, and got upon the flat top of the wall at the bottom of the wood. From here they looked down into Mr. McGregor's garden. Peter's coat and shoes were plainly to be seen upon the scarecrow, topped with an old tam-o-shanter of Mr. McGregor's.

LITTLE Benjamin said, "It spoils people's clothes to squeeze under a gate; the proper way to get in, is to climb down a pear tree."

Peter fell down head first; but it was of no consequence, as the bed below was newly raked and quite soft.

IT had been sown with lettuces. They left a great many odd little foot-marks all over the bed, especially little Benjamin, who was wearing clogs.

LITTLE Benjamin said that the first thing to be done was to get back Peter's clothes, in order that they might be able to use the pocket-handkerchief.

They took them off the scarecrow. There had been rain during the night; there was water in the shoes, and the coat was somewhat shrunk.

Benjamin tried on the tam-o-shanter, but it was too big for him.

THEN he suggested that they should fill the pocket-handkerchief with onions, as a little present for his Aunt.

Peter did not seem to be enjoying himself; he kept hearing noises.

BENJAMIN, on the contrary, was perfectly at home, and ate a lettuce leaf. He said that he was in the habit of coming to the garden with his father to get lettuces for their Sunday dinner.

(The name of little Benjamin's papa was old Mr. Benjamin Bunny.)

The lettuces certainly were very fine.

PETER did not eat anything; he said he should like to go home. Presently he dropped half the onions.

LITTLE Benjamin said that it was not possible to get back up the pear tree, with a load of vegetables. He led the way boldly towards the other end of the garden. They went along a little walk on planks, under a sunny red-brick wall.

The mice sat on their door-steps cracking cherry-stones; they winked at Peter Rabbit and little Benjamin Bunny.

PRESENTLY Peter let the pocket-handkerchief go again.

THEY got amongst flower-pots, and frames and tubs; Peter heard noises worse than ever, his eyes were as big as lolly-pops!

He was a step or two in front of his cousin, when he suddenly stopped.

THIS is what those little rabbits saw round that corner!

Little Benjamin took one look, and then, in half a minute less than no time, he hid himself and Peter and the onions underneath a large basket . . .

THE cat got up and stretched herself, and came and sniffed at the basket.

Perhaps she liked the smell of onions!

Anyway, she sat down upon the top of the basket.

SHE sat there for *five hours*.

*

I cannot draw you a picture of Peter and Benjamin underneath the basket, because it was quite dark, and because the smell of onions was fearful; it made Peter Rabbit and little Benjamin cry.

The sun got round behind the wood, and it was quite late in the afternoon; but still the cat sat upon the basket.

At length there was a pitter-patter, pitter-patter, and some bits of mortar fell from the wall above.

The cat looked up and saw old Mr. Benjamin Bunny prancing along the top of the wall of the upper terrace.

He was smoking a pipe of rabbit-tobacco, and had a little switch in his hand.

He was looking for his son.

OLD Mr. Bunny had no opinion whatever of cats.

He took a tremendous jump off the top of the wall on to the top of the cat, and cuffed it off the basket, and kicked it into the green-house, scratching off a handful of fur.

The cat was too much surprised to scratch back.

When old Mr. Bunny had driven the cat into the green-house, he locked the door.

Then he came back to the basket and took out his son Benjamin by the ears, and whipped him with the little switch.

Then he took out his nephew Peter.

THEN he took out the handkerchief of onions, and marched out of the garden.

WHEN Mr. McGregor returned about half an hour later, he observed several things which perplexed him.

It looked as though some person had been walking all over the garden in a pair of clogs — only the foot-marks were too ridiculously little!

Also he could not understand how the cat could have managed to shut herself up *inside* the green-house, locking the door upon the *outside*.

WHEN Peter got home, his mother forgave him, because she was so glad to see that he had found his shoes and coat. Cotton-tail and Peter folded up the pocket-handkerchief, and old Mrs. Rabbit strung up the onions and hung them from the kitchen ceiling, with the bunches of herbs and the rabbit-tobacco.

THE END